Beyond the Impossible – Doors of Opportunity

This is a work of fiction. Similarities to real people, places, or events are entirely coincidental.

BEYOND THE IMPOSSIBLE – DOORS OF OPPORTUNITY

First edition. October 26, 2024.

Copyright © 2024 Smita Singh.

ISBN: 979-8227659392

Written by Smita Singh.

Preface

In a world that constantly evolves, where new opportunities arise at every turn, it's easy to feel like we're held back by limits—whether imposed by society, circumstance, or even our own minds. How many times have we heard, "It's impossible," or "That can't be done," only to later witness someone else do it, shattering preconceived notions of what's achievable?

This book, *Beyond the Impossible – Doors of Opportunity*, was born out of a fascination with the human spirit's ability to defy limitations. It explores the journey of those who refused to accept the word "impossible" and instead turned that belief into an opportunity. The characters you will meet are not just figures in a story; they represent a piece of all of us. They are the dreamers, the risk-takers, and those who dared to believe that something more was waiting on the other side of a closed door.

In writing this book, my goal is to inspire you, the reader, to reframe how you see obstacles and challenges in your life. Impossibility is not a dead end; it's an invitation. Each challenge you face has the potential to become a stepping stone toward growth and discovery, if only you allow yourself to see the door in the wall before you.

I hope this book serves as a reminder that within every challenge lies a chance to grow, learn, and rise above. The opportunities you seek are out there; sometimes, it's simply a matter of believing in them—and in yourself—enough to open the door.

Thank you for embarking on this journey with me. May you find the inspiration to unlock your own doors of opportunity.

Introduction

We live in a world that often defines us by what we can or cannot do. From the moment we start forming our first dreams, we're met with opinions, limitations, and even well-meaning advice telling us what is realistic. These voices tend to shape our understanding of the word "impossible." Over time, many of us start to internalize these beliefs, letting them dictate the direction of our lives and the scope of our aspirations.

But what if we looked at the concept of "impossible" differently?

When I set out to write *Beyond the Impossible – Doors of Opportunity*, I wanted to challenge the very idea that something can truly be impossible. I realized that many of the most transformative moments in history, and even in our own personal lives, happened when people dared to question what they were told couldn't be done. It's not just about extraordinary talents or resources; it's about a shift in mindset.

Think about a door. A door can be seen as a barrier, preventing you from seeing what's on the other side. Or, it can be an invitation—a challenge that asks you to open it, to step into the unknown and discover what lies beyond. Throughout life, we encounter countless doors that seem locked by circumstance, fear, or doubt. But what if those doors are not as impenetrable as they seem?

In this book, you'll follow the journeys of individuals who faced doors marked "impossible." Through their stories, I want to show you that there is always a way forward, even when it feels like the odds are stacked against you. Each character you meet will be at a crossroads, grappling with their own limitations, doubts, and fears. But through courage, determination, and a belief in the possibilities beyond the impossible, they will each discover new opportunities they hadn't imagined.

My hope is that by the time you finish reading this book, you'll look at your challenges with a new perspective, one filled with hope, potential, and the knowledge that the doors you face are there to be opened.

The Door of Possibility
Chapter 1: The Locked Gate – Anna's Leap of Faith
Chapter 2: The Broken Bridge – Liam's Path to Innovation
Chapter 3: The Stone Wall – Maria's Defiance
Chapter 4: The Shifting Maze – Kaito's Search for Purpose
Chapter 5: The Frozen River – Emily's Quest for Connection
Chapter 6: The Unseen Barrier – Arun's Scientific Breakthrough
Chapter 7: The Endless Desert – Amira's Journey of Faith
Chapter 8: The Silent Mountain – Finn's Battle with Self-Doubt
Chapter 9: The Dark Forest – Alina's Redemption
Chapter 10: The Final Door – The Collective Realization

The Door of Possibility

In the corner of a quiet village, tucked away from the bustling cities and the noise of modern life, there was a place few had ever noticed. It wasn't on any map, and no travel guide had ever written about it. Yet, for those who were lost, confused, or on the verge of giving up, it seemed to appear just when they needed it most.

This place was no grand palace or hidden temple. It was simple—a little cottage perched atop a hill, surrounded by ancient trees whose roots seemed to stretch as deep as the earth itself. But it wasn't the cottage that drew people here, nor was it the beauty of the landscape. It was something far more extraordinary. At the very center of the clearing, just beyond the cottage, stood a door. It was an old, weathered thing made of heavy oak, its surface marked with the cracks and creases of time. There were no walls to hold it up, no house to call its own—just the door, standing alone, with no apparent purpose.

Yet, this door was not ordinary. There was something mysterious about it, something that seemed to beckon those who stood before it. For behind this door lay a secret, one that had the power to change the lives of those who dared to open it. It was the *Door of Possibility*.

The door was not always visible. It appeared only to those who needed it, only to those who stood on the edge of despair or frustration, unable to see the way forward. It appeared to those who had been told that their dreams were impossible, that they would never succeed, that they were not enough. And it was only those people—those brave enough to believe in the impossible—who could unlock the door and step through.

It is said that behind this door lay the answers to all of life's greatest challenges, but not in the way you might expect. The door did not promise riches or fame. It did not guarantee success or instant happiness. What it offered was something far more valuable: the opportunity to see the world differently, to see challenges not as roadblocks but as invitations to grow, to learn, and to push beyond one's limits.

The legend of the Door of Possibility had been passed down through generations, whispered among those who had faced great trials and overcome them. The door, they said, did not appear to everyone. It came only to those who were ready to embrace the unknown, who were willing to face their fears and doubts head-on. And it came at the most unexpected moments—just when all hope seemed lost, when the future looked bleak, and when the weight of the world seemed too much to bear.

The stories of those who had walked through the door were remarkable. They were tales of people who had been told that their dreams were impossible, that they would never achieve what they sought. Yet, by opening the door, they discovered a new path, one that had been invisible to them before. These people—ordinary in many ways but extraordinary in their courage—found a way to push through their limitations and turn their challenges into opportunities.

It was said that the door had appeared to a young artist once, long ago. She had been told her work would never be appreciated, that her vision was too strange, too different. Her family and friends urged her to give up, to find a more practical path. But she could not let go of her passion, no matter how impossible it seemed to succeed. One evening, as she sat in her studio, staring at a blank canvas, the door appeared. Without hesitation, she opened it and stepped through. What she found on the other side was not fame or fortune, but a new perspective, one that allowed her to see her art in a completely different light. She learned to trust her instincts, to follow her heart even when others doubted her. And in time, the world came to see the beauty of her work.

Then there was the story of a young man who dreamed of becoming a doctor. He came from a poor family, with no resources to support his education. Everyone around him told him it was impossible, that he should settle for a simpler life. But deep inside, he knew he was meant for more. One night, as he walked the empty streets of his village, the door appeared before him, glowing faintly in the moonlight. With a trembling hand, he opened it and stepped through. What he found was not a scholarship or a magical solution to his problems, but a new sense of determination and clarity. He realized that the path to his dream was not straightforward, but it was not impossible either. By taking small steps, working harder than ever, and refusing to give up, he eventually achieved what everyone had said was beyond his reach.

And so the stories continued, each one different but connected by the same theme: the door appeared to those who were ready to challenge the notion of impossibility. It appeared to those who had the courage to believe that there was always another way, even when the world told them otherwise.

The Door of Possibility was not just a physical door—it was a symbol, a metaphor for the opportunities that lie hidden within every challenge, every obstacle, every "no" we receive in life. It was a reminder that impossibility is not a fact but a perspective, one that can be changed if we are willing to look beyond the surface.

As the stories of the door spread, people began to speak of it as if it were a legend, a myth. Some believed it was real, while others dismissed it as fantasy. But those who had seen the door knew the truth. They knew that it wasn't the door itself that held the power—it was the act of opening it. It was the moment of decision, the willingness to step into the unknown, that transformed lives.

This is where our story begins.

In the pages that follow, you will meet a group of people, each facing their own impossible challenge. They come from different walks of life, each with their own dreams, struggles, and fears. But they all have one thing in common: they stand before the Door of Possibility, unsure whether to open it. Some of them will hesitate, afraid of what lies on the other side. Others will rush forward, eager to embrace whatever comes their way. But all of them will be changed by what they find.

Our guide through this journey is a wise narrator, a figure who has seen the door appear many times throughout history. This narrator has witnessed the triumphs and the failures, the moments of doubt and the bursts of courage that define the human experience. And now, the narrator invites you, the reader, to follow along as these stories unfold.

The door is not just for the characters in this book. It is for you, too.

As you read, I invite you to consider the doors in your own life. What challenges are you facing that seem impossible? What dreams have you set aside because the path forward seems too difficult? The Door of Possibility is always there, waiting for you to see it. But it is up to you to open it.

Remember, impossibility is an illusion. It is a wall we build in our minds, brick by brick, until we convince ourselves that there is no way through. But beyond that wall is a door, and beyond that door is a world of opportunity, waiting to be discovered.

The choice is yours: Will you open the door?

Chapter 1: The Locked Gate – Anna's Leap of Faith

Anna never thought her life would turn out like this. Born and raised in a quiet, unremarkable town, she had long accepted that the rhythms of her life would forever be dictated by routine. Every day, the same: waking up to the hum of the alarm clock, the scent of freshly brewed coffee filling the small kitchen of her modest apartment, and the slow walk to the office where she worked as an assistant in a law firm. It wasn't that her job was terrible or her life particularly difficult, but the monotony of it all gnawed at her, slowly suffocating the vibrant dreams she had once carried in her heart.

Anna had always wanted to be an artist. Since she was a child, she would spend hours sketching in the backyard, her mind wandering to worlds of color and creativity. Her drawings had filled notebooks, and her room had been a gallery of her imagination. But over time, as the practicalities of adulthood set in, her dreams of becoming an artist seemed to drift further and further away. The harsh reality of paying bills, earning a steady income, and the quiet doubts whispered by others had dulled her once vivid ambition.

"Nobody makes a living as an artist, Anna," her mother had said one evening over dinner. "It's a hobby, not a career. You need something stable."

"Why don't you just paint for fun? Keep it as something you enjoy on the side," her friends would suggest kindly, though their words carried an underlying tone of dismissal, as if they were gently encouraging her to grow out of her childish fantasies.

And so Anna did as everyone expected. She let her dreams of becoming an artist fade into the background. Her paints, once so frequently used, gathered dust in a corner of her closet, and the vibrant canvases she had once loved to fill with color lay forgotten. But something inside her still ached for more. She wasn't sure what it was—a longing, a restlessness—but every day, the feeling grew stronger, as if her soul was reminding her of the life she was meant to live.

The town Anna lived in was small and insular, surrounded by rolling hills and quiet forests. Everyone knew everyone, and little ever changed. It was a place where people settled into their routines early and seldom ventured beyond the familiar. There was something comforting about the predictability, but there was also something stifling about it. For Anna, it felt like a cage.

One evening, as the sun began to sink low on the horizon, casting a golden glow across the rooftops, Anna decided to go for a walk to clear her mind. She needed to escape the confines of her apartment and the crushing weight of her everyday life. She wandered aimlessly through the town, her feet guiding her to a part of it she rarely visited—the outskirts, where the town met the woods. Here, the houses were fewer, and the sounds of nature took over, with the whisper of the wind through the trees and the distant call of birds filling the air.

As she walked further, something caught her eye—something she had never noticed before. Hidden behind overgrown bushes and twisted vines was an old, weathered gate. It stood alone, its rusty hinges and faded wood showing signs of age and neglect. The gate led to nowhere in particular; beyond it, the forest seemed thick and untamed, and from what Anna could tell, no one had used it in years, if not decades. The path to it was barely visible, swallowed by the wild growth of the woods.

Intrigued, Anna stopped and stared at the gate for a long moment. She had lived in this town her whole life, yet she had never noticed this gate before. There were no signs, no markers, and no one had ever mentioned it. It was as if it had been forgotten, left behind by time itself.

"What's behind there?" she wondered aloud. "Why has no one opened it?"

Her curiosity grew. The gate seemed out of place, like a secret waiting to be uncovered. Something about it called to her, tugging at a part of her that had long been dormant—the part of her that still believed in possibility, in adventure, in taking risks.

For days, Anna couldn't stop thinking about the gate. She passed by it on her walks, lingering longer each time. The more she looked at it, the more her curiosity turned into a quiet longing. It was irrational, she knew. It was just an old gate, likely leading to nothing but overgrown woods. But something about it stirred her soul.

The gate became a symbol in her mind—a barrier between her current life and something more. It represented the unknown, the possibility of something different, something beyond the ordinary. Yet, with that possibility came fear. What if opening the gate led to nothing? What if it was a waste of time? What if it made no difference at all?

The "what ifs" paralyzed her. It was the same fear that had kept her from pursuing her art, the same fear that had convinced her to stay in a job that didn't fulfill her. The unknown was terrifying, and stepping into it required faith—a faith that had been worn down by years of practicality and compromise.

Still, every time she thought about giving up the idea of opening the gate, a voice inside her whispered, "What if this is your chance? What if this is the moment that changes everything?"

Anna knew that if she didn't open the gate, she would always wonder. She would always question what lay beyond it, just as she had always questioned what her life could have been if she had followed her passion for art. And so, despite the fear, despite the doubts that clawed at her, she made a decision.

One evening, with the moon hanging high in the sky and the town quiet beneath its silver light, Anna found herself standing in front of the gate once again. This time, she was ready. She had brought a small flashlight, a pair of gloves, and enough courage to push through her fear.

Taking a deep breath, she reached out and touched the old wood. It was rough under her fingers, weathered by time and the elements. The gate creaked slightly as she pressed her hand against it, as if it had been waiting for this moment just as long as she had.

With a firm grip, Anna pushed the gate open.

At first, nothing seemed different. The forest on the other side was dark and thick, the trees standing like silent sentinels. But as she stepped through, something inside her shifted. The air felt different—lighter, more alive. It was as if she had crossed an invisible threshold, moving from one reality to another.

Anna's heart raced. She wasn't sure where she was going, but she knew she had to keep moving forward. The path, though overgrown, seemed to beckon her deeper into the woods. She followed it, her flashlight illuminating the way. Each step felt like a journey into the unknown, but with every step, her fear lessened, replaced by a growing sense of excitement.

As she walked, the memories of her lost dreams flooded back to her. She remembered the joy she had once felt when she painted, the way the world seemed to come alive through her art. She remembered the ambitions she had buried under practicality and the hopes she had abandoned in favor of stability.

But now, walking through this mysterious forest, Anna felt those dreams stirring once again. It was as if the gate had unlocked something inside her—something she had long forgotten. The fear of failure, of the unknown, began to fade, replaced by the realization that the only real failure was never trying at all.

After what felt like hours of walking, Anna emerged into a small clearing. The trees parted, and in the center of the clearing stood an old, abandoned cabin. It was simple, with a thatched roof and wooden beams, but there was something magical about it. The cabin seemed to glow in the moonlight, as if it had been waiting for her arrival.

Anna approached the cabin cautiously, her heart pounding with anticipation. As she reached the door, she hesitated for a moment before turning the handle and pushing it open. Inside, the cabin was empty, except for a single easel standing in the center of the room. On the easel was a blank canvas, and beside it, a set of paints and brushes, waiting to be used.

Tears welled up in Anna's eyes as she realized what she had found. This was her moment—her chance to start again. The gate had not led her to a magical solution or an easy answer. Instead, it had led her back to herself, to the dreams she had once abandoned but had never truly lost.

With trembling hands, Anna picked up a brush and dipped it into the paint. As she placed the brush against the canvas, the world seemed to fall away. Time slowed, and all that existed was the paint, the canvas, and the art that flowed from her heart. For the first time in years, Anna felt truly alive.

That night, as Anna painted in the little cabin, she realized that the gate had been more than just a physical barrier. It had been a symbol of her fear—her fear of the unknown, of failure, of stepping outside the life she had built for herself. But by opening the gate, by taking that leap of faith, she had discovered something far more important: the power of possibility.

Life, Anna realized, is full of gates—gates that we often ignore because we are too afraid to open them. We convince ourselves that it's safer to stay where we are, to stick to what we know, even if it means living a life that doesn't fulfill us. But the truth is, the only thing holding us back is our fear.

Anna's journey through the gate wasn't just a journey into the woods; it was a journey into herself. It was a reminder that the first step is always the hardest, but once you take it, the possibilities are endless. The fear of the unknown is real, but it is not insurmountable. And sometimes, all it takes is a leap of faith to unlock a world of opportunity.

As the sun began to rise, casting a warm glow over the forest, Anna knew that her life would never be the same. She had opened the gate, both literally and metaphorically, and there was no turning back. The future was uncertain, but for the first time in a long time, that uncertainty felt exciting rather than terrifying.

She smiled to herself as she packed up her paints and began the journey home, knowing that this was only the beginning. The locked gate had been her barrier, but now, it was her gateway to a new life—one filled with creativity, possibility, and the courage to pursue her dreams.

In the end, Anna learned that fear is the true barrier to possibility, not reality. The gate had always been there, waiting to be opened, just as her dreams had always been within reach. It was her fear of the unknown that had kept her trapped in a life of routine and complacency. But by taking that first step, by opening the gate, she had unlocked not only a new path but also a new understanding of herself.

Anna's story is a reminder that the greatest risks often lead to the greatest rewards. The unknown can be daunting, but it is also full of opportunity. And sometimes, all it takes is the courage to take the first step, to open the gate, and to trust that the journey ahead will be worth it.

Chapter 2: The Broken Bridge – Liam's Path to Innovation

Liam stared out of his apartment window, watching the futuristic city hum with life below. The skyline was dotted with towering skyscrapers made of gleaming glass and metal, and sleek, silent vehicles zipped along the airways, leaving trails of light in their wake. It was a city built on progress, where technology had advanced so far that problems of the past seemed irrelevant. Yet despite all this progress, one problem remained unsolved: how to cross the canyon.

The canyon had been there for as long as anyone could remember—a massive, jagged scar on the earth, separating the city from the vast lands beyond. No one could live near it, let alone cross it, because the canyon was notorious for its dangerous winds and volatile weather patterns. Any attempt to build a bridge had ended in disaster. The city's best engineers had tried for decades, only to be thwarted by nature's fury. Liam had been one of those engineers, and after numerous failures, he was ready to give up.

Liam's latest attempt had been a disaster. His design for a high-tech suspension bridge, reinforced with the strongest materials available, had collapsed spectacularly during a test run. The winds had ripped it apart, sending it crashing into the depths of the canyon. His peers had rejected his ideas, calling them impractical and overly ambitious. He had become the laughingstock of the engineering community, a once-promising innovator now labeled as someone who couldn't deliver.

Sitting in his small, cluttered apartment, Liam felt the weight of his failures pressing down on him. Blueprints were scattered across his desk, crumpled and covered in red marks from the reviews of his colleagues. His dreams of revolutionizing the city's infrastructure now seemed impossible. He had poured years of his life into the project, only to watch it fall apart, literally and figuratively.

The bridge had become an obsession for Liam. It wasn't just about solving an engineering problem anymore; it was about proving to himself and everyone else that he could do it. But after countless failures, he was beginning to wonder if the project was simply impossible. The canyon was too wide, the winds too strong, the environment too hostile. No matter how advanced the city's technology became, it seemed like nature had the upper hand.

His colleagues had given up long ago, turning their attention to more achievable projects—new transportation systems, energy-efficient buildings, and the like. But Liam couldn't let go of the bridge. He had grown up hearing stories about the lands beyond the canyon, about the untapped resources and opportunities that lay on the other side. If only there were a way to get there, the city could expand and thrive like never before. It was more than just a bridge—it was a gateway to the future.

But after his most recent failure, even Liam's optimism had begun to wane. He had gone over the design a hundred times, trying to figure out where he had gone wrong. He had used the best materials, accounted for the weather conditions, and followed every engineering principle he knew. Yet the bridge had collapsed, just like all the others. What was he missing?

One evening, after another long day of trying and failing to make sense of his designs, Liam found himself standing at the edge of the canyon. The wind howled through the air, swirling dust and debris around him. He stared out into the void, the vast emptiness stretching before him, and felt a pang of hopelessness. Maybe it really was impossible.

The thought of giving up gnawed at him. He had dedicated years of his life to this project, but at what cost? His reputation was in shambles, his relationships had suffered, and he hadn't slept properly in weeks. The weight of his failures was crushing, and for the first time, he considered walking away.

"Maybe it's time to move on," he muttered to himself, the words tasting bitter in his mouth. But even as he said it, he knew it wasn't what he wanted. He didn't want to quit, but he couldn't see a way forward.

Disheartened, Liam made his way back into the city, his thoughts a jumble of frustration and defeat. As he walked through the bustling streets, he couldn't help but feel disconnected from the world around him. Everyone else seemed to be moving forward, while he was stuck, unable to solve the one problem that mattered most to him.

Later that night, unable to sleep, Liam decided to take a walk to clear his mind. The city's libraries were open 24/7, offering a quiet refuge for those seeking knowledge or simply a place to think. He wandered into one of the older libraries, a grand, imposing building filled with dusty tomes and forgotten records. It wasn't a place most people visited anymore—most information was digital now—but there was something comforting about the physical presence of books.

Liam wandered the aisles aimlessly, running his fingers along the spines of old engineering textbooks, historical accounts, and theoretical papers. He wasn't looking for anything in particular, just a distraction from the gnawing sense of failure that had taken hold of him.

As he rounded a corner, something caught his eye—an old, leather-bound book, partially hidden behind a stack of newer volumes. It looked ancient, the edges of the pages yellowed with age. Curious, he pulled it off the shelf and examined the cover. The title was barely legible, but he could make out the words: *Innovations of the Past: Forgotten Engineering Marvels.*

Intrigued, Liam flipped open the book and began to read. It was a collection of blueprints and designs from centuries ago, many of which had never been built or had been lost to time. The drawings were rough, the language outdated, but as Liam turned the pages, he felt a spark of inspiration. These engineers had faced challenges just as difficult as his—bridges over impassable rivers, buildings in earthquake-prone areas—and yet they had thought outside the box, creating solutions that were ahead of their time.

As he neared the end of the book, Liam's eyes widened. There, nestled among the final pages, was a blueprint for a bridge. But it wasn't like any bridge he had ever seen. Instead of relying on suspension cables or traditional supports, this design used a series of interconnected arches, anchored deep into the canyon walls. The arches were flexible, designed to move with the wind rather than resist it, allowing the bridge to withstand the violent gusts that had destroyed all previous attempts.

Liam's heart raced as he studied the design. It was so different from anything he had ever considered, yet it made perfect sense. The problem wasn't that the canyon was impossible to cross—it was that he had been approaching it the wrong way. He had been trying to build a bridge that fought against the forces of nature, rather than working with them.

Liam hurried back to his apartment, the old blueprint clutched in his hands. He spent the entire night poring over the design, sketching out modifications and adapting it to modern technology. The more he worked, the more excited he became. This was it—the breakthrough he had been waiting for. The design wasn't perfect, but it was a starting point, a new way of thinking about the problem.

Over the next few days, Liam threw himself into the project with renewed energy. He used the blueprint as inspiration, but he also added his own innovations, incorporating advanced materials and technology that hadn't existed when the original design was created. He ran simulations, tested different models, and consulted with experts in various fields. Slowly but surely, the pieces began to fall into place.

The design wasn't just about building a bridge—it was about rethinking the entire approach to engineering in hostile environments. Liam realized that innovation often came from failure, from pushing the boundaries of what was known and daring to try something different. His previous designs had failed because he had been too rigid in his thinking, too focused on traditional methods. But now, by embracing a new perspective, he was able to see possibilities where before there had only been obstacles.

With his new design in hand, Liam knew it was time to face his peers again. Despite his excitement, he couldn't shake the lingering fear of rejection. His colleagues had already dismissed him once, and his reputation was still tarnished by his previous failures. But this time felt different. He had something truly groundbreaking, and he believed in it with every fiber of his being.

The day of the presentation arrived, and Liam stood before a room full of skeptical engineers and city planners. He could feel their eyes on him, waiting for him to fail again. But as he unveiled the new design, something shifted in the room. The skepticism began to fade, replaced by curiosity and even admiration.

Liam explained the concept behind the flexible arches, how they would allow the bridge to move with the wind rather than resist it. He demonstrated the advanced materials that would give the structure strength and flexibility, and he showed simulations of the bridge standing firm even in the most extreme conditions.

When he finished, there was a moment of silence. Then, slowly, the room erupted in applause. His peers, the same ones who had doubted him for so long, were now praising his innovation. They could see the potential in his design, the way it redefined what was possible.

For the first time in months, Liam felt a sense of accomplishment. He had done it. He had taken the failures of the past and turned them into the foundation for something new, something revolutionary.

The city approved Liam's design, and construction began shortly thereafter. It wasn't an easy process—the canyon was still a treacherous environment, and there were countless challenges along the way. But Liam was no longer discouraged by setbacks. He had learned that failure was simply part of the journey, a necessary step on the path to innovation.

Months later, the bridge stood completed, a sleek, elegant structure stretching across the canyon. It was unlike any bridge the city had ever seen, a testament to the power of creativity and perseverance. As Liam stood at the edge of the canyon, watching the first vehicles cross the bridge, he felt a deep sense of pride. He had not only solved the problem—he had redefined what was possible.

Liam's journey was one of overcoming failure and adapting to new challenges. The broken bridges of his past had not been the end of the road, but rather the beginning of a new way of thinking. Through persistence and creativity, he had turned failure into an opportunity for growth.

Innovation often comes from the willingness to embrace failure, to learn from it, and to keep moving forward. Liam's story is a reminder that what seems broken can always be mended with creativity and new perspectives. The key is not to give up, but to keep pushing the boundaries of what is possible, even when the path ahead seems uncertain.

In the end, Liam had not just built a bridge—he had built a legacy of innovation, proving that even the most daunting challenges can be overcome with the right mindset and a willingness to take risks.

Chapter 3: The Stone Wall – Maria's Defiance

Maria stood at the edge of the forest, her eyes fixed on the towering stone wall that loomed in the distance. It was ancient, its surface weathered by centuries of rain, wind, and time. Stories told of how the wall had stood since the beginning of the kingdom, built to keep out enemies during times of war. Now, it served as a boundary, both literal and metaphorical, between the wild, untamed forest and the structured, rigid world of the kingdom.

In many ways, Maria felt a kinship with the wall. Like her, it stood alone, defiant, and unmoving in the face of opposition. And like the wall, Maria had spent her life confronting an unyielding force: tradition.

The kingdom of Arion was a place where tradition reigned supreme. For centuries, it had followed the same customs and rules, handed down from one generation to the next. There were strict roles for men and women, expectations that dictated how one should live, work, and behave. Men were warriors, leaders, and protectors. Women were caregivers, homemakers, and scholars—but only in certain approved subjects.

Maria had always been different. From a young age, she had felt the pull of a life that went beyond the constraints of her gender. While other girls played with dolls and practiced their stitching, Maria spent her days watching the royal guard train in the courtyard. She marveled at the way they moved, their swords gleaming in the sunlight as they practiced their drills. She longed to be one of them, to wield a sword and protect the kingdom from threats. But that dream, she was told, was impossible.

"No woman has ever been a warrior," her father had said time and again, his voice heavy with resignation. "It's not the way of things, Maria. You must accept your place."

Her mother had been no different, urging her to focus on her studies and her future as a scholar. "You have a brilliant mind," her mother had said, pride in her voice. "You'll make a name for yourself in the libraries, perhaps even as a royal advisor one day."

But that wasn't what Maria wanted. She respected knowledge and scholarship, but her heart burned with a desire for more. She didn't just want to learn about history—she wanted to make it. She didn't just want to read about warriors—she wanted to be one. But every time she spoke of her dream, she was met with the same dismissive responses: "It's not possible." "Women don't fight." "You'll never break the rules of tradition."

The stone wall had become a symbol for Maria. Hidden deep within the forest, it was said to be unbreakable, built by ancient kings to protect the kingdom from invaders. Over the years, it had become a legend, a place that children whispered about and adventurers sought to challenge, only to return defeated. No one had ever broken through the wall. But Maria wasn't deterred by the stories. She saw the wall as more than just a physical barrier—it was a representation of the societal limits that had been placed on her.

One day, after another heated argument with her family about her desire to join the royal guard, Maria had stormed out of the house and found herself at the edge of the forest. Without thinking, she had followed the narrow path that led deeper into the woods, her feet carrying her to the base of the stone wall. She had stood there, staring up at the towering structure, her mind racing.

"I'll break through," she had whispered to herself, her voice barely audible over the rustling of the trees. "If no one else can, I will."

From that day forward, Maria returned to the wall every chance she got. She trained relentlessly, not just in mind but in body, honing her strength and stamina. She studied combat techniques in secret, borrowing books from the royal library and practicing with wooden swords she had crafted herself. She trained under the cover of darkness, away from prying eyes, and her determination grew with every passing day.

But it wasn't enough just to train. Maria knew that if she was ever going to prove herself, she had to break through the wall. It had become her personal challenge, a test of her strength and resilience. The wall represented everything that had been denied to her—the chance to fight, the chance to defy expectations, the chance to be something more than what society allowed.

At first, her attempts were feeble. She had tried to scale the wall using ropes and hooks, only to find the stone too smooth, the surface too high. She had tried to dig beneath it, but the foundation ran deep into the earth, unyielding. She had even tried using her knowledge of engineering to devise a way to weaken the structure, but the wall had stood firm.

Each failure left her more determined. It wasn't just about the wall anymore—it was about proving to herself, and to the world, that she wouldn't be stopped by something as simple as tradition. The wall was a challenge, yes, but it was also a reminder of the barriers that society had placed in her path. And if she could break through this wall, maybe she could break through those barriers too.

As the weeks turned into months, Maria's secret journey became more difficult to keep hidden. Her absences from home were noticed by her family, and her friends began to ask questions about where she disappeared to for hours at a time. The whispers of doubt and disapproval grew louder, and soon, Maria found herself at odds with those she loved most.

"You're wasting your time," her father said one evening, his voice tinged with frustration. "No one can break through that wall. It's been there for centuries, Maria. Do you think you're the first to try?"

Her mother, ever the voice of reason, tried to appeal to her logic. "Why do you insist on this foolishness? You have a future ahead of you as a scholar. The royal court is always in need of advisors with your intelligence. Why throw that away for a dream that will never come true?"

But Maria couldn't explain it to them. She couldn't put into words the fire that burned inside her, the need to prove herself not just to the kingdom, but to herself. It wasn't just about the wall—it was about everything the wall represented. The doubts, the limitations, the expectations that had been placed on her since birth. She couldn't accept a life where she was told what she could and couldn't do, simply because of who she was.

One evening, after yet another argument with her father, Maria stormed into the forest with renewed determination. She had reached her breaking point. She couldn't continue living in a world where her dreams were dismissed as impossible. She had to break through, not just for herself, but for every woman who had ever been told that she wasn't enough.

As she stood before the wall, her heart pounding in her chest, Maria felt a surge of defiance unlike anything she had ever felt before. She wasn't going to back down. She wasn't going to accept the limits that had been placed on her. She was going to break through.

With a deep breath, Maria charged at the wall. She struck it with all her strength, her fists pounding against the stone. The impact reverberated through her body, but she didn't stop. Again and again, she struck the wall, her knuckles bleeding, her muscles screaming in protest. But she refused to give up. She had spent her whole life being told what she couldn't do—she wasn't going to let this wall, or anyone else, stop her.

Hours passed, and Maria continued her relentless assault on the wall. Sweat poured down her face, mixing with the blood on her hands, but she didn't care. She was fighting for something greater than herself. She was fighting for her right to dream, to challenge the rules, to defy expectations.

As the night wore on, Maria's strength began to wane. Her vision blurred, and her body screamed for rest. But just as she was about to collapse from exhaustion, something incredible happened. A crack appeared in the wall.

At first, it was barely noticeable—a thin, jagged line running down the surface of the stone. But as Maria stared at it, disbelief and hope surged through her. She had done it. She had made a crack.

With renewed energy, Maria struck the wall again, her fists slamming into the stone with all the force she could muster. The crack widened, and with each blow, the wall began to crumble. The unbreakable wall, the one that had stood for centuries, was falling apart before her eyes.

Finally, with one last, desperate strike, the wall collapsed. Dust and debris filled the air, and Maria staggered back, her body trembling with exhaustion. But as the dust settled, she saw what lay beyond the wall: a path, winding through the forest and disappearing into the horizon. A path that no one had ever seen before.

When Maria returned to the kingdom, word of her achievement spread like wildfire. The story of the young woman who had broken through the unbreakable wall became a symbol of defiance, of courage, and of the power to challenge societal expectations. The royal court, once so rigid in its traditions, was forced to reconsider its rules. For the first time in history, women were allowed to train as warriors, inspired by Maria's unyielding determination.

Maria herself was invited to join the royal guard, and though the path ahead was still filled with challenges, she knew that she had already won the greatest battle of all: the battle against the limitations that others had placed on her. She had proven that what others deemed impossible was simply a barrier waiting to be broken.

Maria's journey was not just about breaking through a wall—it was about breaking through the invisible barriers that society had built around her. The wall had been a symbol of tradition, of the rules and expectations that had confined her, but Maria's determination and courage had shown that no barrier is truly unbreakable.

Challenging societal expectations requires more than just physical strength—it requires the strength of spirit, the belief in oneself, and the willingness to defy the rules that others accept without question. Maria's story is a reminder that what seems impossible is often only impossible because no one has dared to try.

In the end, Maria had not just broken a wall—she had broken a legacy of limitation, proving that courage and persistence are the true keys to change. The kingdom would never be the same, and neither would Maria.

Chapter 4: The Shifting Maze – Kaito's Search for Purpose

Kaito stood at the entrance of the labyrinth, his heart pounding as he gazed into the seemingly endless maze. The stone walls loomed high above him, twisting and turning in unpredictable patterns, shrouded in mist that made it impossible to see more than a few feet ahead. The path before him looked straightforward, but he had been warned: nothing in this maze was as it seemed.

In a kingdom filled with tradition and certainty, Kaito had always felt out of place. He was different from others his age—where they saw clear paths laid out for their futures, Kaito only saw fog. While his friends chose their roles—scholars, merchants, warriors—Kaito found himself questioning what his purpose in life truly was. What was he meant to do? Where was he meant to go? Every decision seemed fraught with uncertainty, every path unclear. The Shifting Maze had appeared in his dreams, a labyrinth that reflected his inner turmoil, and when the invitation came to enter it in real life, Kaito couldn't resist.

He had heard tales of the maze from the village elders—stories of people who had entered but never returned. Some said the maze was cursed, a place designed to trap the lost and confused. Others claimed it was a test of one's character, a place where those seeking answers could find their true purpose. But no one truly knew what lay within the maze, and that was what intrigued Kaito the most. It was the unknown—the same unknown that mirrored his life—and he was determined to find clarity.

The air inside the maze was thick and heavy, as if it held secrets of its own. Kaito took a deep breath, squaring his shoulders as he stepped

forward. The path ahead seemed clear, a straight line leading into the mist, but he knew better than to trust his first impression.

As he walked, he felt the walls shifting around him, as if the maze itself was alive, responding to his movements. At first, it was subtle—a slight change in the angle of the path, a shift in the ground beneath his feet. But soon, the changes became more dramatic. The walls would close in on him, forcing him to turn back, or they would stretch into impossibly long corridors that seemed to have no end. It didn't take long for Kaito to lose his sense of direction.

At each turn, the maze seemed to mock him. He'd walk confidently down one path, only to find it had twisted back on itself. Every step felt like a misstep. The maze was in constant flux, and no matter how hard he tried, Kaito couldn't get his bearings.

After what felt like hours of wandering, Kaito came across his first companion in the maze. The man was sitting against a wall, his clothes tattered and his face gaunt. His eyes were hollow, and his expression was one of resignation.

"Are you lost too?" Kaito asked, his voice hoarse from the silence.

The man looked up, his eyes devoid of hope. "There is no way out," he muttered. "I've been here for years, searching for an exit. It doesn't exist. The maze changes too quickly, and the paths are never the same. There's no point in trying."

Kaito frowned, feeling a knot of frustration in his chest. "But there has to be a way," he insisted. "Why else would the maze exist if not for us to find a way through?"

The man let out a bitter laugh. "That's what I thought too, when I first entered. But you'll see soon enough. The maze doesn't care about your determination or your effort. It's designed to keep you wandering forever."

With those words, the man slumped back against the wall, his spirit broken. Kaito felt a wave of doubt wash over him. Was this what his future held? Endless wandering, with no purpose or direction? Was the maze truly unbeatable, just like the uncertainties of his life?

But something inside him rebelled against the idea. He wasn't ready to give up, not yet. The maze might shift, the walls might change, but that didn't mean there wasn't a lesson to be learned. Maybe the point wasn't to find a way out—maybe the point was to keep moving, to keep searching.

Determined not to let despair take hold, Kaito continued his journey through the maze. As he walked, he encountered others who had also become lost. Some had given up entirely, sitting in corners of the maze with blank expressions, waiting for an exit that would never come. Others wandered aimlessly, too afraid to make decisions or choose a path, fearing that every choice would lead to failure.

Kaito spoke with many of them, listening to their stories. He realized that each person had entered the maze searching for something—answers, purpose, direction—but had become trapped by their own fears and uncertainties. The shifting walls had broken their spirits, convincing them that the maze was unbeatable.

But Kaito refused to accept that. He continued to explore, making note of the patterns in the maze's shifts. He observed the way the walls moved, the way certain paths closed off and others opened. Slowly, he began to see a rhythm in the chaos, a pattern in the unpredictability. The maze was alive, yes, but it wasn't impossible to navigate. It required a different way of thinking—a willingness to adapt, to embrace the uncertainty rather than fight against it.

As Kaito journeyed deeper into the maze, something shifted within him. The frustration and fear he had felt at the beginning began to fade, replaced by a sense of calm. The maze no longer felt like an enemy, but a challenge—one that required patience, observation, and adaptability. He realized that the more he tried to control the maze, the more lost he became. But when he let go of his need for control, when he allowed himself to flow with the changes rather than resist them, the path became clearer.

He stopped searching for a fixed exit and instead focused on navigating the present moment. The maze was always shifting, but that didn't mean it was impossible to move forward. It required flexibility and an open mind—qualities that Kaito had been lacking in his life outside the maze. He had spent so long searching for a clear path, for a definite purpose, that he had forgotten how to embrace the unknown.

It was during one of these moments of clarity that Kaito came across something unexpected—a small, ancient stone altar in the center of the maze. Upon it rested a single, unlit lantern. The sight of it stopped him in his tracks.

The lantern felt significant, though Kaito didn't know why. He approached it cautiously, reaching out to touch its cool surface. As his fingers brushed against it, the lantern flickered to life, casting a warm, golden glow across the maze.

With the light of the lantern, the maze no longer seemed so intimidating. The walls still shifted, but the path ahead was more discernible. Kaito could see further, navigate more easily. It was as if the light had unlocked a new level of understanding, allowing him to see the maze for what it truly was—a test of persistence, not a trap.

As Kaito continued his journey with the lantern in hand, he realized that the maze hadn't been about finding an exit at all. It had been about learning to navigate the unknown, to adapt to change, and to find clarity in confusion. The maze, like life, was full of uncertainties—unexpected turns, dead ends, and shifting paths—but that didn't mean it was hopeless. It required resilience, flexibility, and, above all, faith in oneself.

The lantern had not shown Kaito the way out of the maze; instead, it had illuminated the path ahead, helping him see that the journey itself was the purpose. He no longer felt the need to find an exit. He no longer feared the shifting walls or the uncertainty of his future. Instead, he embraced the journey, confident that each step forward, no matter how uncertain, was leading him to greater understanding.

Along the way, Kaito encountered others still wandering in the maze. Some were hesitant to follow him, still clinging to their belief that the maze was a trap with no way out. But others saw the light of the lantern and joined him, inspired by his determination and clarity. Together, they navigated the shifting paths, learning from one another and growing stronger with each step.

After what felt like an eternity of wandering, Kaito reached the heart of the maze. It wasn't an exit, as he had once expected, but a vast open space, filled with light and warmth. The walls, once oppressive and confining, had receded, revealing a horizon that stretched endlessly into the distance.

In that moment, Kaito understood. The maze had never been about finding an exit. It had been about learning to navigate uncertainty, about finding purpose in the journey rather than the destination. The shifting walls, the dead ends, the moments of doubt—they had all been part of the lesson.

Kaito looked around at the others who had joined him on the journey. Each of them had faced their own fears and uncertainties, but together, they had found clarity. They had learned that life, like the maze, was full of shifting paths and unknowns, but that didn't make it hopeless. It made it an adventure.

With a deep breath, Kaito smiled. He had found his purpose—not in the certainty of a single path, but in the willingness to embrace the unknown and navigate it with courage and resilience.

Kaito's journey through the Shifting Maze was a reflection of the uncertainties we all face in life. The maze, with its constantly changing walls and unpredictable paths, symbolized the confusion and doubt that often accompany our search for purpose. But Kaito's story teaches us that clarity doesn't come from avoiding uncertainty—it comes from embracing it.

Life is full of shifting paths, dead ends, and moments of doubt, but that doesn't mean we should give up. Like Kaito, we must learn to adapt, to let go of our need for control, and to trust in our ability to navigate the unknown. The true purpose of the maze was not to find an exit, but to find meaning in the journey itself.

In the end, Kaito didn't need to escape the maze—he needed to learn how to navigate it. And in doing so, he discovered that the journey was the purpose all along.

Chapter 5: The Frozen River – Emily's Quest for Connection

The wind howled through the village of Frostvale, carrying with it a chill that seemed to pierce the bones. Emily stood by her window, gazing at the bleak, snow-covered landscape that stretched as far as the eye could see. The village had been blanketed in an unforgiving cold for as long as she could remember. Winters were harsh in Frostvale, and this year, the village felt even more cut off from the world. The river that bordered the town had frozen solid, and the snow piled so high it had become impossible to leave or receive supplies from the neighboring villages. The townsfolk said it was a curse of nature, one they had no choice but to endure.

But for Emily, the frozen river felt like more than just a physical barrier. It was symbolic of the isolation and loneliness she had felt her entire life. She had always lived on the fringes of her community, unsure of her place, believing that she had little to offer. In a village where people prided themselves on their ability to survive the harsh winters, she felt inadequate and disconnected. Every person had a role—the hunters, the healers, the builders. But Emily felt she had none. Her heart ached with a desire for connection, yet she found herself retreating further into solitude, convinced that she had nothing to contribute.

As she stared at the frozen river, Emily made a decision. This winter, she would no longer remain passive, trapped by both the icy landscape and her own self-doubt. The village needed help, and if no one else was willing to venture beyond the frozen river, then she would. She would find a way across and bring back supplies, proving to herself and the village that she was capable of more than they thought. Little did she know, this journey would teach her far more than how to cross the river—it would reveal her own strength, resilience, and the power of human connection.

The isolation of Frostvale was not just a product of its geography—it was also an emotional isolation that ran deep within its inhabitants, especially Emily. The long winters, where daylight was fleeting and the cold seeped into every corner, created a sense of detachment in the villagers. People spoke only when necessary, rarely venturing out of their homes unless they had a task to perform. Relationships were functional, with little room for warmth or intimacy. And for Emily, who had always been shy and withdrawn, this environment only heightened her sense of alienation.

She remembered growing up feeling like an outsider even among her peers. While other children laughed and played in the snow, Emily had been more interested in books and her own thoughts. Her parents were loving but distant, preoccupied with their own struggles to keep the household running through the harsh winters. And as she grew older, Emily found it increasingly difficult to connect with others. Her quiet nature was often mistaken for aloofness, and soon people stopped trying to include her in their conversations or gatherings. It wasn't that they were cruel—they simply didn't know how to reach her, and Emily didn't know how to reach them.

For years, she convinced herself that she was fine being alone. She didn't need the village's approval, nor did she need friends. But deep down, she knew that wasn't true. The loneliness gnawed at her, especially in the long, dark winters when the cold seemed to freeze not just the river but also the hearts of the people around her.

The morning Emily decided to embark on her quest was bitterly cold, the frost clinging to the trees like skeletal hands. She wrapped herself in layers of fur and wool, preparing for the harsh conditions she would face. The villagers thought she was mad when she announced her plan.

"You'll freeze out there," one of the elders warned. "That river's been frozen for weeks, and no one's made it across. You're risking your life."

"The river's impossible to cross," added another villager. "It's too dangerous."

But Emily shook her head. "We can't just sit here waiting for the snow to melt. We need supplies, and no one's coming to help us. If I don't go, who will?"

Despite their protests, no one stepped forward to join her. The fear of the unknown, of the biting cold and treacherous ice, kept the villagers in their homes. Even her family tried to dissuade her, but Emily had made up her mind. For too long, she had let fear and self-doubt dictate her life. This time, she would be brave.

With a bag of provisions and a small sled to carry supplies back, she set off toward the river. As she walked through the village, she felt the weight of the villagers' eyes on her. They watched in silence, perhaps judging her or perhaps silently hoping she would succeed where they had given up. But as soon as she stepped beyond the last row of houses, the village disappeared from view, swallowed by the swirling snow.

The river loomed ahead, a vast expanse of ice and snow. The once mighty waterway that had brought life and trade to the village was now a frozen wasteland, its surface slick and treacherous. Emily stood at its edge, her breath coming in short, sharp bursts as she surveyed the scene. The wind whipped through her hair, and for a moment, she felt a pang of doubt. Was this really possible? Could she really make it across? But she had come too far to turn back now.

Stepping onto the ice, she tested its strength. The surface groaned beneath her weight, but it held. She took another step, and then another, each one feeling more uncertain than the last. The ice was unpredictable, with cracks and fissures hidden beneath the snow. But Emily moved forward, her determination pushing her beyond her fear.

As she walked, the cold began to seep into her bones. The air was frigid, and even her thick layers of clothing offered little protection. Her fingers and toes went numb, and every breath she took burned in her chest. The landscape around her was desolate, a sea of white with no landmarks to guide her. The village was long out of sight, and ahead lay only more ice and snow.

About halfway across the river, the ice beneath Emily's feet began to shift. She heard a sharp crack, and before she could react, the ground gave way. Her heart raced as she plunged into the freezing water, the cold shock hitting her like a wall. Instinctively, she kicked and struggled, her hands clawing at the ice to find something to hold onto. The icy water was like knives against her skin, and panic surged through her.

For a moment, it seemed as though the river would claim her. But Emily refused to give up. Gritting her teeth against the cold, she reached for a nearby chunk of ice and hauled herself up, gasping for air as she scrambled back onto solid ground. Her clothes were soaked, and the cold clung to her like a second skin, but she was alive.

Shivering uncontrollably, Emily knew she couldn't stop now. If she stayed still, the cold would take her. She had to keep moving, had to find a way to dry herself off and get warm. With her fingers numb and clumsy, she fumbled with her pack, pulling out a small tinderbox and some dry kindling. It took several attempts, but eventually, she managed to start a small fire on the ice.

The warmth of the flames was a lifeline, and as she sat by the fire, Emily felt a surge of gratitude. She had survived. The frozen river had tried to stop her, but she had fought back. And in that moment, something shifted inside her. She wasn't the weak, helpless girl she had always believed herself to be. She had strength, resilience, and a will to survive.

Once she had warmed herself and her clothes had dried enough to continue, Emily resumed her journey across the river. Every step felt like a battle against the elements—the ice beneath her feet, the wind biting at her face, and the cold seeping into her bones. But she pressed on, fueled by a new sense of determination.

As she walked, Emily thought about the village she had left behind. The people of Frostvale had always kept to themselves, isolated not only by geography but by choice. They had built walls around themselves, both physically and emotionally, and Emily realized that she had done the same. She had let her fear of rejection and her feelings of inadequacy keep her from connecting with others. But now, as she ventured into the unknown, she understood that true strength didn't come from isolation. It came from connection—from reaching out, even when it was difficult, and from believing that she had something valuable to offer.

The river was a barrier, yes, but it was also an opportunity. It was a challenge that forced her to confront her fears and push beyond the limits she had set for herself. And as she neared the far side of the river, Emily knew that crossing it was only the beginning.

When Emily finally reached the opposite bank, the sun was beginning to set, casting a pale, golden light over the snow-covered landscape. She stood for a moment, gazing back at the frozen river that had seemed so impossible to cross. It was still the same river, still just as cold and unforgiving, but something had changed. Emily no longer saw it as an insurmountable obstacle. She had crossed it, and in doing so, she had proven to herself that she was capable of more than she had ever imagined.

The journey had been difficult, but it had also been transformative. Emily had faced her fears, battled the elements, and survived. She had discovered her own strength and resilience, and along the way, she had learned the importance of connection—not just with others, but with herself.

As she made her way toward the neighboring village, Emily felt a new sense of purpose. She was no longer the isolated, uncertain girl who had left Frostvale. She was a survivor, a warrior, and someone who had something valuable to offer the world. And when she returned to her village, she would bring not only the supplies they needed but also a message of hope and resilience.

The frozen river had tried to stop her, but Emily had crossed it. And in doing so, she had crossed the invisible barriers she had built within herself. The journey had changed her, and she knew that the next time she faced an obstacle—whether physical or emotional—she would be ready to face it with courage and determination.

Emily's journey across the frozen river is a metaphor for the internal battles we all face. The feelings of isolation, self-doubt, and inadequacy can freeze us in place, just as the river had frozen her village. But by daring to venture into the unknown, by facing her fears head-on, Emily discovered her own strength and resilience.

The lesson of the frozen river is that our greatest obstacles are often the ones we create for ourselves. The walls of isolation and self-doubt that we build can be just as impenetrable as the ice that covered the river. But by reaching out to others, by believing in our own worth, and by refusing to give in to fear, we can break through those barriers and find the connection and purpose we seek.

In the end, Emily's quest was not just about crossing a frozen river. It was about discovering her own power, learning the value of community, and realizing that she had something valuable to offer the world. And in doing so, she became a beacon of hope for her village, showing them that even in the coldest, most isolated places, there is always a way forward.

Chapter 6: The Unseen Barrier – Arun's Scientific Breakthrough

Arun stood before the cluttered desk in his small, dimly lit laboratory, the hum of various machines filling the air. The flickering glow of a single lamp illuminated his worn-out notebooks, filled with scribbles, equations, and diagrams that seemed to come alive in the half-light. He rubbed his tired eyes, pushing his round glasses up the bridge of his nose, and stared down at the pages. These were not just numbers and symbols—they were the keys to a reality that no one else seemed to believe existed. Arun's heart pounded with a mixture of excitement and apprehension. He was on the brink of something extraordinary, something that could change the world forever.

But outside the walls of his lab, society held a different view. In Arun's world, curiosity was viewed with suspicion, and certain fields of study were considered dangerous, bordering on heresy. Quantum physics was at the top of that list. The leaders of his society had long declared that the mysteries of the quantum realm were beyond human comprehension and that any attempt to understand them would lead to disaster. "The unseen forces that govern the universe are not for us to tamper with," they said. "Some barriers are meant to remain intact."

Arun, however, refused to accept that. From a young age, he had been fascinated by the intricacies of the universe—the way light could behave both as a particle and a wave, the peculiar behavior of atoms and subatomic particles, and the strange, invisible forces that seemed to weave the fabric of reality together. These mysteries weren't barriers; they were invitations. And though his colleagues and mentors warned him to abandon his pursuits, Arun's curiosity burned too brightly to be extinguished.

Tonight, after years of secret study and experimentation, he was closer than ever to a discovery that could shatter the limits of knowledge imposed by his society. He was on the verge of uncovering a new form of energy, one that could revolutionize science, technology, and the very way people understood the universe.

The world Arun lived in wasn't one of ignorance. It was a society that prided itself on progress, on the achievements of the past, and the mastery of well-understood science. But it was also a society governed by caution, where certain areas of inquiry were considered too dangerous, too unknown. There had been a time, centuries ago, when the pursuit of knowledge knew no bounds—when scientists and thinkers delved fearlessly into the mysteries of existence. But those days were long gone.

According to the ruling council, which dictated the boundaries of acceptable knowledge, there were certain truths that humans were not meant to uncover. "The unseen barriers of the universe are not to be breached," they warned. "Tampering with forces we do not understand will only lead to chaos and destruction."

Quantum physics, with its strange paradoxes and counterintuitive truths, was seen as the most dangerous of all. While basic physics and classical mechanics were embraced, the more abstract and theoretical realms—those that ventured into the quantum—were considered taboo. The idea that particles could exist in multiple states at once, that they could communicate across vast distances instantaneously, or that the act of observation could change reality itself—these concepts were seen as too disruptive to the natural order.

Arun had grown up hearing these warnings, but he had always been different. While others feared the unknown, he was drawn to it. As a child, he had spent hours gazing at the stars, wondering what lay beyond the limits of human understanding. He read every book he could find on the subject, even those banned by the council.

BEYOND THE IMPOSSIBLE – DOORS OF OPPORTUNITY

And when he became a scientist, he knew that his true calling lay in exploring the very areas that others avoided.

The "unseen barrier" that his society spoke of was not a physical one, but a mental and philosophical one. It was a barrier created by fear—fear of the unknown, fear of change, fear of what lay beyond the comfortable boundaries of their current understanding. Arun knew that to break through this barrier, he would need more than just equations and experiments. He would need the courage to challenge the limits of knowledge itself.

Arun's lab was small, hidden in the basement of an old, crumbling building on the outskirts of the city. It was here, far from prying eyes, that he had spent the last several years conducting his experiments in secret. His colleagues thought he was a fool for pursuing quantum physics, and his mentors had long since given up on trying to dissuade him. "You're chasing ghosts," they said. "The quantum world is beyond our reach. It's a realm of chaos and unpredictability."

But Arun knew better. He believed that the chaos they feared was simply a lack of understanding. The universe operated by laws, even if those laws were beyond the grasp of conventional thinking. If he could just find the right key, the right perspective, he could unlock a new level of reality.

His research had started innocently enough—basic quantum experiments that had been conducted in secret by the few renegade scientists before him. He had replicated the famous double-slit experiment, observing the wave-particle duality of light. He had explored the concept of quantum entanglement, where particles seemed to communicate instantaneously, defying the limitations of space and time. But these were just the beginning. Arun was after something bigger.

Over the years, he had developed a hypothesis about a new form of energy—a quantum energy that existed in the fabric of space itself.

It wasn't like conventional energy sources, such as electricity or nuclear power. This energy was woven into the very structure of reality, and if harnessed, it could provide limitless power, revolutionizing technology, transportation, and communication.

But there was a problem. No one had ever observed this energy directly. It was purely theoretical, a concept that existed only in the equations and in Arun's mind. And without proof, Arun knew that his society would never accept it.

One night, after weeks of relentless work and sleepless nights, Arun found himself on the edge of a breakthrough. He had constructed a new device—an intricate, delicate machine designed to detect the quantum fluctuations that might reveal the presence of this new energy. It was a risky experiment. If the machine failed, it could set his research back months, or even years. But Arun was out of time. The ruling council had begun to suspect his activities, and he knew that if they discovered what he was working on, they would shut him down permanently.

With trembling hands, he activated the machine. For several minutes, nothing happened. The hum of the machinery filled the room, and the tiny lights on the device flickered faintly. Arun's heart raced as he watched the monitors, searching for any sign of a fluctuation. Time seemed to stretch out endlessly, and doubt began to creep into his mind. What if he had been wrong all along? What if this energy didn't exist?

And then, just as he was about to lose hope, the monitors flashed. A spike. It was small, almost imperceptible, but it was there. Arun's eyes widened as he watched the data stream in. The spike grew larger, more defined, and soon it became clear: the energy was real. It wasn't just a theoretical construct—it was a tangible, measurable force.

Arun felt a surge of triumph. This was the proof he had been searching for. He had broken through the unseen barrier that his society had constructed, and in doing so, he had opened the door to a new era of science and discovery.

But Arun's breakthrough came at a cost. No sooner had he celebrated his discovery than he heard the sound of footsteps outside his lab. The ruling council had been watching him more closely than he had realized. The door burst open, and several council members entered, their faces stern and disapproving.

"Arun," the leader of the council said, "we warned you. This research is dangerous. You have tampered with forces beyond your understanding."

Arun stood his ground. "I understand more than you think," he said, his voice steady. "This energy is real. It's not dangerous—it's the key to a new future."

But the council members were unmoved. "You have violated the laws of our society," the leader said. "Knowledge like this comes with consequences. You've seen the chaos that can result from meddling with the unknown."

Arun knew that they were referring to the disaster that had occurred centuries ago when unchecked scientific experimentation had led to the collapse of civilizations. But he also knew that fear had kept them from seeing the potential for progress. "This energy isn't chaos," he argued. "It's the answer to our problems. It could provide limitless power, solve our energy crisis, and push the boundaries of what we can achieve. We can't let fear hold us back."

The council, however, was not willing to listen. They ordered Arun to dismantle his machine and destroy his research. They warned him that if he continued down this path, he would face severe punishment.

But Arun couldn't give up. He had seen what was possible, and he knew that the future of science depended on pushing past the limits of fear and ignorance. He made a choice that night—a choice to continue his work in secret, despite the risks.

Arun's discovery, though kept hidden from the public, began to ripple through the scientific community. A few trusted colleagues who shared his passion for knowledge and progress quietly supported his work, helping him refine his theories and expand his experiments. Together, they developed new technologies that could harness the quantum energy Arun had discovered.

Though the council tried to suppress his findings, the truth could not be contained. Word spread, and soon other scientists began to question the limits imposed by the council. The fear that had once kept them in line began to crumble, replaced by a renewed sense of curiosity and wonder.

Arun's breakthrough became the catalyst for a new scientific revolution. Over time, the council's grip on knowledge weakened, and society began to embrace the pursuit of understanding once again. The unseen barrier that had held them back for so long had finally been breached.

Arun's journey was not just a scientific breakthrough—it was a testament to the power of curiosity and the pursuit of knowledge. The unseen barrier that his society had constructed was not a physical one, but a mental one—a barrier of fear and ignorance that kept people from exploring the unknown.

The lesson of Arun's story is that just because something hasn't been done before doesn't mean it's impossible. Curiosity, innovation, and the desire to understand the world can break through even the most entrenched barriers. By challenging the limits of knowledge, Arun not only discovered a new form of energy but also helped his society move past its fear of the unknown.

In the end, Arun's story is a reminder that progress comes from those who dare to ask questions, to challenge the status quo, and to push beyond the boundaries of conventional thinking. The unseen barrier may seem impenetrable, but with courage, determination, and an unwavering belief in the power of knowledge, it can be broken. And once it is, the possibilities are endless.

Chapter 7: The Endless Desert – Amira's Journey of Faith

The harsh sun blazed overhead, casting waves of heat across the endless stretch of sand. The desert seemed eternal, an unforgiving landscape with no end in sight. To the casual observer, it was a barren wasteland, void of hope and life. But to Amira, the desert was more than just a physical place—it was a reflection of the struggles she carried within her soul.

Amira, a young nomad of the Desertwind tribe, stood on the crest of a sand dune, her eyes scanning the horizon. She knew every grain of sand in this desolate place, having been born into the nomadic life that defined her people. Her tribe had roamed these lands for generations, moving with the rhythms of nature, living in harmony with the desert's harsh beauty. But now, the rhythms had changed. The once-reliable rains had stopped, and the waterholes that sustained them had dried up. The drought had stretched on for months, and the tribe's survival was at stake.

The elders of the tribe, wise in their years, had gathered the people and declared that there was no hope. "The desert has swallowed all the oases," they said. "The water has vanished, and so will we. Our journey is at its end." Their words weighed heavily on the tribe. Some resigned themselves to their fate, while others prayed for rain that never came.

But Amira refused to accept their grim prophecy. Deep within her heart, a small flicker of hope remained. She couldn't shake the feeling that there was something more, something unseen beyond the horizon. Call it instinct or faith, but Amira believed there was still an oasis waiting to be found, hidden deep within the desert's endless expanse.

One evening, as the tribe huddled around a meager fire, Amira approached her father, Malik, one of the tribe's elders. His

once-strong face was lined with worry, his hands shaking from the effort of rationing what little water remained.

"Father," Amira said softly, "I want to go out into the desert. There must be an oasis somewhere. I can find it."

Malik's face darkened with concern. "Amira, you know what the elders have said. There is no oasis. The desert has turned against us."

"But I feel it," she insisted. "I can't explain it, but I know there's something out there. I have to try."

Her father sighed, staring into the fire. "The desert is vast and dangerous, Amira. We have lost too many to the sands. If you leave, you may never return."

"I'm willing to take that risk," Amira said, her voice steady with resolve. "If I don't go, we'll die here anyway. I'd rather die searching for hope than sit and wait for the end."

Malik looked at his daughter with a mixture of pride and fear. He saw the determination in her eyes, the same determination he had once felt in his youth. He knew that nothing he said would stop her. With a heavy heart, he placed a hand on her shoulder.

"Go then," he said quietly. "But take this with you." He handed her a small, worn leather pouch—the tribe's last supply of water. "It's all we have left. Use it wisely."

Amira nodded, her throat tight with emotion. She hugged her father one last time, then turned away from the fire and the faces of her tribe, setting her sights on the darkening horizon. The desert awaited.

Amira's journey began in darkness. The coolness of the desert night was a brief reprieve from the scorching heat of the day, but the landscape was no less treacherous. She walked through the night, her feet sinking into the soft sand with each step, her mind racing with doubts. What if the elders were right? What if there was no oasis? What if she was chasing a mirage, a phantom born of desperation?

But as the first light of dawn crept over the horizon, illuminating the vast sea of dunes, Amira pushed those thoughts aside. She had made her decision, and there was no turning back. She would trust her instincts, trust the journey, and believe in the unseen oasis that she knew was out there.

The first day passed slowly, the sun rising higher and higher in the sky, its heat relentless. Amira shielded her face with a scarf, but the heat still beat down on her, sapping her strength. By midday, she had only taken a few sips from her water pouch, but her throat was parched, and her lips cracked from the dryness. Still, she pressed on.

As the day wore on, the desert played its tricks on her mind. The heat blurred the horizon, making it seem as though pools of water shimmered in the distance. But Amira knew better. These were nothing but mirages, cruel illusions cast by the desert to taunt the weary traveler. She ignored them, focusing on the steady rhythm of her footsteps and the pulse of hope that still beat within her.

As night fell again, the temperature plummeted, and the desert winds began to howl. Amira wrapped her thin cloak tighter around her body, seeking warmth. The cold was just as brutal as the heat, and the biting wind cut through her clothing like shards of ice. But she refused to stop. She knew that if she rested, if she allowed herself to succumb to the fatigue, she might never rise again.

On the second day, the trials of the desert became more severe. Her water supply was dwindling, and the sun's merciless rays bore down on her with renewed intensity. The blisters on her feet had worsened, and each step sent a jolt of pain up her legs. Her muscles ached, her vision blurred, and her mind grew foggy from exhaustion and dehydration.

But Amira refused to give in. She knew that if she faltered now, it would all be for nothing. She thought of her tribe, of her father, and of the hope that she carried with her. This was not just her journey—it was theirs as well. They were counting on her, even if they didn't know it.

As the day dragged on, Amira stumbled upon a jagged outcropping of rocks. Desperate for shade, she crawled beneath them, her body trembling with fatigue. She closed her eyes, her thoughts drifting. The image of her tribe appeared in her mind—her father's face, the elders, the children who played in the sand despite the drought. They were all waiting for her. They needed her to find the oasis. She couldn't let them down.

Suddenly, her eyes snapped open. The sun was setting, and with it came the danger of the cold desert night. She had to keep moving, no matter how much her body protested.

By the third day, Amira's strength was nearly gone. Her water pouch was empty, and her body was weak from thirst. Her lips were cracked and bleeding, and her vision had begun to blur again. Every step was a monumental effort, and yet, she kept going.

Her mind wandered in and out of consciousness, her thoughts fragmented and scattered. She found herself questioning everything. Had she been foolish to believe in an oasis? Was this journey nothing more than a delusion born of desperation? The elders had warned her, after all. Perhaps they were right. Perhaps there was no oasis, no hope. Perhaps the desert had truly won.

But then, a small voice inside her, faint but unwavering, reminded her of why she had set out in the first place. It was faith—not in the oasis, but in herself. She had trusted her instincts, trusted the journey, and that was all she had left. Even if the oasis didn't exist, her faith was real. And that was enough.

As she walked, she began to notice something strange. The desert around her had changed. The sand dunes were no longer as steep, and the wind, though still present, had softened. There was a different scent in the air, one that she hadn't noticed before. It was faint, but it was there—the smell of water.

Her heart leaped, and with renewed energy, she quickened her pace. She followed the scent, her instincts guiding her. Every step was painful, her body on the verge of collapse, but she kept moving forward. She had come too far to stop now.

And then, as she crested one final dune, she saw it.

It was real.

Before her, nestled in a small valley between the dunes, was a lush oasis. Palm trees swayed gently in the breeze, their leaves casting dappled shadows on the sparkling blue water below. Birds circled overhead, their calls echoing across the desert. The sight was so beautiful, so surreal, that Amira thought she might be dreaming. But the cool breeze that brushed against her sunburned skin told her otherwise.

Tears welled in her eyes as she stumbled down the dune, her legs shaking with exhaustion. She fell to her knees at the edge of the water, cupping her hands and drinking deeply. The water was cool and sweet, filling her with a sense of relief so profound that it brought her to tears.

The oasis was real. It had been there all along, hidden just beyond the reach of those who had given up hope. Amira had found it—not through maps or logic, but through faith. She had trusted herself, trusted the journey, and it had led her to salvation.

Amira rested at the oasis for several days, regaining her strength. The water and the shade of the palm trees rejuvenated her, and soon she was ready to return to her tribe. She filled several water skins from the oasis and set out across the desert once more, this time with a heart full of hope.

When she finally returned to her tribe, the sight of her alive and well, carrying the water from the oasis, brought tears to their eyes. She had defied the odds, defied the elders, and saved them all.

Amira's journey through the endless desert was more than a physical trial—it was a test of faith. The desert represented the obstacles and doubts that we all face in life, the moments when the path ahead seems uncertain and hope feels distant. But Amira's story teaches us that no matter how endless the desert may seem, there is always an oasis ahead if we keep moving forward.

Faith is not always about knowing the destination; sometimes, it's about trusting the journey. Amira didn't know where the oasis was, or even if it existed, but she believed in herself and in the possibility of something more. Her perseverance, even in the face of exhaustion and doubt, is a reminder that the most important journey we take is the one within ourselves.

The lesson of Amira's story is clear: sometimes the journey is long and difficult, but faith and perseverance can lead us to places we never imagined. Life may feel like an endless desert, but if we trust the path we are on and believe in our own strength, we can find the oasis waiting for us just over the next dune.

Chapter 8: The Silent Mountain – Finn's Battle with Self-Doubt

The world of towering peaks and boundless skies was once Finn's domain. As a seasoned mountaineer, he had spent years chasing the thrill of scaling the world's most challenging mountains. He had climbed cliffs of ice, crossed treacherous crevasses, and stood on summits that seemed to touch the heavens. But all of that felt distant now—like memories from a different life.

Finn sat at the base of a massive mountain known only as "The Silent Mountain." It loomed above him, its icy peaks disappearing into the clouds, casting an ominous shadow over the valley below. Its name wasn't just a reference to the quiet stillness that enveloped it, but to the legends that surrounded it. No one had ever successfully reached its summit. It was said to be impossible, an unforgiving peak that had claimed many lives.

Once, a challenge like this would have excited Finn. He would have felt his pulse quicken, his fingers itch for the feel of cold stone and ice. But now, all he felt was fear. It had been nearly a year since his last climb—the climb that had gone so terribly wrong.

The memory of that fateful day still haunted Finn. It had started out like any other ascent—meticulously planned, every detail accounted for. He and his team had set out to conquer one of the world's most dangerous peaks, full of confidence. But nature had other plans. A sudden avalanche, faster and more violent than anyone had expected, had swept through the slopes, leaving chaos in its wake.

Finn had survived, but not everyone had been so lucky. The guilt of losing his climbing partner, Tom, weighed heavily on him. He had seen Tom disappear beneath the snow, heard his desperate cries for help before everything went silent. Finn had tried to reach him, but the mountain had swallowed him whole. The rescue efforts had been in vain.

After that, something inside Finn had broken. He had sworn off climbing. The once unshakable confidence he had in his abilities had crumbled into dust. The mountains, which had once been his refuge, now seemed like unforgiving monsters, waiting to claim him next.

And yet, here he was, standing at the foot of The Silent Mountain. He wasn't sure why he had come. Perhaps it was out of some twisted sense of duty, or maybe it was a final attempt to face the demons that had chased him for the past year. Either way, he couldn't walk away. Not yet.

The mountain loomed above him, impossibly high and cold, its jagged edges cutting into the sky. Finn could feel the wind howling through the narrow valleys that snaked around its base, as if the mountain itself was breathing, watching, waiting. It was silent, yes, but its presence was deafening.

As Finn stared up at the towering peak, his heart began to race. His hands trembled slightly, the familiar sensation of anxiety creeping into his chest. He tried to shake it off, telling himself that he was prepared, that he had climbed mountains more dangerous than this one. But the voice in the back of his mind, the one that had grown louder since that fateful avalanche, wouldn't let him forget.

"What if you fail again?" the voice whispered. "What if this mountain is your end?"

Finn swallowed hard, pushing the thoughts aside. He had come this far—he couldn't turn back now.

The climb began the next morning. Finn set out before dawn, the air frigid and still. His breath formed clouds of condensation in the early morning light, and the crunch of snow beneath his boots was the only sound that accompanied him.

He moved slowly at first, each step deliberate, as if testing the mountain's resolve. The early stages of the climb were deceptively easy, with gentle slopes and firm ground beneath his feet. But Finn knew better. The real challenge lay ahead.

As he ascended higher, the landscape became more treacherous. The snow deepened, the slopes grew steeper, and the wind picked up, howling through the narrow passes. The biting cold gnawed at his skin, and the air grew thinner, making it harder to breathe. But these were obstacles he had faced before. The real challenge was the battle raging inside him.

With every step, Finn could feel the weight of his doubts pressing down on him. His mind was a battlefield, torn between the part of him that had once been fearless and the part of him that had been shattered by the avalanche. Every time he looked up at the mountain, it seemed to grow taller, more impossible.

As the day wore on, fatigue began to set in. The climb became more technical, with narrow ledges and sheer cliffs that required every ounce of focus and skill. Finn found himself gripping the rock tighter than necessary, his hands trembling with a mix of exertion and fear. The wind tugged at his jacket, trying to pull him off balance, and the snow-covered cliffs made every step feel precarious.

At one point, he reached a narrow ridge, a sheer drop on either side. His heart raced as he inched forward, his body pressed flat against the cold rock. He could feel the wind tugging at him, and for a moment, he froze. Memories of the avalanche flooded his mind—the sensation of the ground giving way beneath him, the terror of being buried alive. His breathing grew shallow, and his vision blurred. Panic gripped him.

"You can't do this," the voice whispered again. "You're going to fall."

Finn clenched his teeth, his body trembling with fear. He wanted to turn back, to abandon the climb and retreat to the safety of the base. But something stopped him. A different voice—fainter, but steadier—spoke up inside him.

"Keep going."

It was the voice of the climber he had once been, the part of him that believed in himself, that trusted in his abilities. He forced himself to take a deep breath, to focus on the next step, the next handhold. Slowly, he moved forward, inch by inch, until he reached the other side of the ridge.

As Finn continued his ascent, the mountain threw its worst at him. A sudden snowstorm swept in, reducing visibility to near zero. The wind howled, and the temperature plummeted. He huddled behind a boulder, waiting for the storm to pass, but the cold seeped into his bones, and his muscles ached from the strain.

He felt the old fear rising again—the fear that he wasn't strong enough, that the mountain would claim him just as it had claimed so many others. But this time, something was different. This time, he didn't run from the fear. Instead, he faced it head-on.

He closed his eyes, focusing on his breathing, calming his racing heart. The storm raged around him, but inside, Finn found a stillness. He realized that the fear he felt wasn't a weakness. It was a part of him, just as much as his strength and skill. He couldn't ignore it, but he could choose not to let it control him.

When the storm finally passed, Finn rose to his feet, his body sore and exhausted, but his mind clearer than it had been in a long time. He looked up at the peak, still far above him, and took a deep breath. He could do this. He would do this.

The final stretch of the climb was the most challenging yet. The slopes grew steeper, the air thinner. His muscles screamed in protest, and his lungs burned with every breath. But Finn pressed on, one step at a time.

The summit was close now, tantalizingly within reach. But the closer he got, the more his doubts tried to resurface. What if he slipped? What if the mountain defeated him at the last moment?

But Finn had learned something important along the way. The mountain wasn't his true enemy. His real battle was with himself—with the fear, the guilt, and the self-doubt that had haunted him since the avalanche.

As he neared the summit, Finn paused, looking out at the vast expanse of snow and sky. He realized that the journey had never been about conquering the mountain. It had been about conquering the doubts that had held him back for so long. The mountain was a mirror, reflecting his inner struggle. And now, standing on the brink of the summit, he knew that he had already won.

With a final burst of strength, Finn climbed the last few meters and pulled himself onto the summit. He stood there, breathless, as the wind whipped around him, the world stretching out in every direction beneath him. The view was breathtaking, but what filled him with the most pride was the knowledge that he had faced his fears and emerged stronger.

As Finn stood on the summit of The Silent Mountain, he realized that the greatest battle he had faced wasn't against the elements or the mountain itself—it had been against his own mind. The fear and self-doubt that had plagued him for so long had been his real enemies. And now, standing at the top of the world, he knew that he had finally conquered them.

The journey down the mountain was easier, not because the terrain had changed, but because Finn had changed. He had learned to trust himself again, to believe in his abilities, and to face his fears head-on. The Silent Mountain had taught him that the barriers we face in life are often the ones we create for ourselves. And by breaking through those barriers, we can achieve things we once thought were impossible.

Finn's battle with The Silent Mountain wasn't just about climbing a peak—it was about facing the inner demons that had been holding him back. The mountain represented the challenges we all face in life, the obstacles that seem insurmountable. But Finn's story teaches us that the greatest barriers are often the ones we place on ourselves.

Self-doubt, fear, and guilt are powerful forces, but they are not insurmountable. By confronting these emotions and refusing to let them control us, we can achieve things we never thought possible. Finn's journey is a reminder that the true battle is always within, and that by conquering our inner demons, we can conquer the world around us.

The Silent Mountain may have been a physical challenge, but its true lesson lies in the strength of the human spirit. Just as Finn learned to trust himself again, we too can find the strength to overcome our fears and reach new heights—both in the mountains and in life.

Chapter 9: The Dark Forest – Alina's Redemption

The village of Eirendale had once flourished under the leadership of Alina, a young woman whose wisdom and strength had made her the pride of her people. She had been chosen as the head of the council at a time when her village needed her most. With her bold decisions and innovative ideas, she had led them through many crises—famine, drought, and even invasions from neighboring territories. But all of her accomplishments felt like distant memories now.

Alina's fall from grace had been swift and devastating. A single mistake—one fatal decision—had changed everything. It had been a time of great uncertainty when she had chosen to expand the village's borders in search of more resources. But this expansion had angered the spirits of the forest, entities that the villagers had long respected and feared. Her decision had caused great harm, sparking a curse that brought sickness, starvation, and despair to her people.

The village had turned against her, blaming her for the suffering they now faced. Once their beloved leader, Alina had become a pariah. The guilt weighed heavily on her heart, and the once-confident woman now lived in constant shame. In the eyes of the villagers, she was the source of their misery, and no one believed she could redeem herself.

And so, with a broken spirit and heavy heart, Alina had left the village, retreating into the Dark Forest, a place where it was said no one ever returned. The Dark Forest, thick with ancient trees and an unsettling silence, was feared by all who lived in Eirendale. It was a place of myth and legend, where it was said that those who entered were never seen again. But Alina didn't care. She felt that she deserved whatever fate awaited her there.

The air was thick and still as Alina stepped into the forest, the towering trees closing in around her. The light of the sun was quickly swallowed by the dense canopy above, leaving her in near-total darkness. A deep silence permeated the forest, broken only by the occasional rustle of leaves or the distant cry of an unseen creature. It was a place of eternal twilight, where shadows seemed to move of their own accord.

As she ventured deeper into the forest, Alina felt a strange sense of calm wash over her. The fear that others felt about the forest didn't seem to grip her in the same way. Perhaps it was because she had already lost everything, and there was little left to fear. Or perhaps, somewhere deep inside, she believed that this dark, foreboding place was where she was meant to be—where she could confront the mistakes of her past.

Her footsteps were slow and deliberate as she walked through the undergrowth, each step echoing in the quiet darkness. Her mind raced with thoughts of the past—memories of the village before the curse, of the people who had once trusted her, and of the decisions that had led to her downfall. It was as if the forest itself was forcing her to confront the weight of her guilt, to face the consequences of her actions.

As night fell, Alina found a clearing deep within the forest. A small fire crackled in front of her, casting flickering shadows on the trees that loomed around her like silent sentinels. The flames brought little comfort. The forest remained oppressive, its darkness ever-present, as if it was waiting for something—some acknowledgment or revelation from her.

Sitting by the fire, Alina's mind was a whirlwind of emotions—regret, sorrow, anger, and shame. The weight of her past actions felt like a physical burden, one that had driven her from her home and her people. She had made a terrible mistake, one that had cost lives and caused her village immense suffering. How could she ever hope to make things right? Could she ever find redemption?

The fire's light danced on the surface of a nearby pool of water, its dark depths reflecting the sky above. Alina rose and walked to the edge of the pool, looking down at her reflection. Her face was pale and drawn, her once-bright eyes now dull with sorrow. She barely recognized the woman staring back at her.

"I've failed," she whispered to herself, her voice barely audible over the crackling fire. "I failed them all."

As she spoke the words aloud, a chill ran down her spine. The forest seemed to close in on her, as if the very trees were listening, judging her. The darkness felt alive, watching, waiting. And then, from the shadows, a voice echoed in the stillness.

"You failed, yes. But failure is not the end."

Alina spun around, startled. Standing at the edge of the clearing was an old woman, cloaked in a robe made of dark, gnarled branches. Her face was lined with age, her eyes sharp and piercing, glowing faintly in the dim light of the fire. She seemed to be a part of the forest itself, an ancient presence that had been there long before Alina had arrived.

"Who are you?" Alina asked, her voice shaking.

"I am the keeper of this forest," the old woman replied, her voice low and steady. "I have seen many souls come here, lost and broken like you. Some seek redemption, others seek oblivion. But tell me, child, what do you seek?"

Alina hesitated. What did she seek? Redemption? Forgiveness? Or perhaps just a way to escape the crushing guilt that had haunted her since the day she had made her fateful decision?

"I don't know," Alina admitted. "I made a mistake—a terrible mistake. I led my people into ruin, and I don't know how to fix it. I don't even know if it can be fixed."

The old woman nodded, as if she had heard these words many times before.

"Redemption is never easy, Alina. It requires great sacrifice. But it is always possible."

The old woman beckoned Alina to follow her deeper into the forest. As they walked, the darkness grew even thicker, and the air became heavy with an oppressive stillness. Alina could barely see the ground in front of her, but the old woman moved with ease, as if she had walked this path many times before.

"Your village is in grave danger," the old woman said after a long silence. "The curse that you unleashed upon them is growing stronger. If nothing is done, it will consume them all."

Alina's heart sank. She had suspected as much, but hearing it confirmed sent a fresh wave of guilt crashing over her.

"But there is a way to save them," the old woman continued. "The spirits of the forest are not vengeful by nature, but they have been wronged. They demand balance. To break the curse, you must restore that balance."

"How?" Alina asked, her voice trembling.

"The forest will test you," the old woman replied cryptically. "You will face trials—trials that will force you to confront the darkness within yourself. Only by overcoming these trials can you hope to find redemption."

Alina felt a knot of fear form in her stomach. She had already been through so much—was she truly strong enough to face whatever trials lay ahead? But she knew she had no choice. If she wanted to save her village, if she wanted to find redemption, she had to continue.

The first trial came in the form of shadows—dark, creeping figures that slithered out of the trees and circled around Alina. They whispered in her ear, their voices cold and cruel, reminding her of her failures, her mistakes, her weaknesses.

"You are nothing," they hissed. "You brought ruin to your people. You are a coward, running away from the consequences of your actions."

Alina felt their words cutting deep, feeding the self-doubt and guilt that had plagued her for so long. The shadows grew darker, their voices louder, until they seemed to be pressing down on her from all sides.

But as the shadows closed in, Alina realized something. These shadows were not real. They were manifestations of her own guilt, her own fear. They had no power over her—unless she let them.

With a deep breath, Alina stood tall and faced the shadows.

"I know I made a mistake," she said, her voice firm. "But I will not let that mistake define me. I will find a way to make things right."

As she spoke the words aloud, the shadows began to fade, their whispers growing fainter until they disappeared completely. Alina had passed the first trial.

The second trial came in the form of a choice. As Alina continued her journey through the forest, she came to a fork in the path. One path was smooth and easy, leading out of the forest and back to safety. The other was treacherous, winding through jagged rocks and dense thorns.

The old woman appeared once again, standing at the fork in the path.

"To save your village, you must choose the difficult path," she said. "It will require great sacrifice, but it is the only way to restore balance."

Alina looked at the two paths and felt the weight of the decision pressing down on her. The easy path was tempting—after all, she had been through so much already. But she knew that taking the easy way out would not lead to redemption. True redemption required sacrifice.

With a deep breath, Alina chose the difficult path.

The journey was long and painful. The thorns tore at her skin, and the rocks bruised her feet. But she pressed on, determined to see it through. Each step was a reminder that redemption was not meant to be easy—it was meant to be earned.

The final trial was the hardest of all. After days of wandering through the forest, Alina found herself standing before a large, ancient tree. Its twisted branches reached up to the sky, and its roots dug deep into the earth. In the center of the tree was a door, glowing faintly with a soft, golden light.

The old woman appeared once more, standing beside the tree.

"To break the curse, you must forgive yourself," she said. "Only by letting go of the guilt that you carry can you find the strength to save your village."

Alina felt tears welling up in her eyes. Forgive herself? How could she possibly do that? She had caused so much harm—how could she ever be worthy of forgiveness?

But deep down, she knew that the old woman was right. She had been carrying the weight of her guilt for so long, and it had consumed her. If she wanted to save her village, she had to let go of that guilt and find the strength to move forward.

With a trembling hand, Alina reached out and touched the door. As she did, a wave of warmth washed over her, and she felt the weight of her guilt begin to lift. It wasn't easy—letting go of her mistakes was the hardest thing she had ever done—but she knew it was the only way.

When Alina emerged from the Dark Forest, she was not the same person who had entered. She had faced her darkest fears, confronted her mistakes, and found a way to forgive herself. The trials of the forest had been difficult, but they had also been necessary.

As she returned to the village, Alina was greeted with wary eyes. The people still remembered her mistakes, but Alina no longer carried the weight of their judgment. She had found a way to break the curse, to restore balance, and to save her people.

Redemption, she realized, was not about erasing the past—it was about learning from it, growing from it, and finding the strength to make things right.

Alina's journey through the Dark Forest teaches us that no mistake is too great to overcome. We all make mistakes, and sometimes those mistakes can have devastating consequences. But redemption is always possible—if we are willing to confront our past, face our inner demons, and make the sacrifices necessary to make things right.

The Dark Forest represents the darkness that we all carry within ourselves—the guilt, the shame, the fear. But just as Alina found her way through the forest, we too can find our way through the darkness. By facing our mistakes, forgiving ourselves, and seeking redemption, we can emerge from the darkness stronger, wiser, and more resilient than before.

In the end, the journey through darkness can lead to the greatest light.

Chapter 10: The Final Door – The Collective Realization

The air was thick with anticipation as the figures stood before the massive, imposing door. It was ancient, carved with intricate patterns and symbols, glowing faintly with a light that seemed to come from within. The door seemed alive, pulsing gently as if waiting for something—or someone—to act. It towered over the group, stretching upwards as far as the eye could see, casting a long shadow across the ground. The figures standing before it represented different walks of life, different journeys, and different lessons learned. Yet, they were united in one purpose: to open the door and step into a future of infinite possibilities.

They were not strangers to one another, though many had never met in the flesh before this moment. They had each faced trials, learned lessons, and had grown along their individual journeys. Some had encountered insurmountable challenges, while others had fallen and risen again. But it was here, at the foot of this monumental door, that their stories converged.

The group was a blend of personalities, each carrying with them the weight of their experiences and the wisdom they had gained. There was Alina, the once-proud leader who had redeemed herself in the Dark Forest; Max, the awkward boy whose first crush had taught him about courage and vulnerability; Mia, who had questioned societal norms and found strength in defiance; and others from the stories that had unfolded throughout the book. Each person carried a vital piece of knowledge, and each was essential to unlocking the door.

As they stood before the door, a deep sense of awe and uncertainty washed over them. It was clear that this was no ordinary door. It was the culmination of all their journeys—the ultimate test of their growth and understanding. To open it, they would need to combine everything they had learned along the way: their courage, their wisdom, and their resilience.

BEYOND THE IMPOSSIBLE – DOORS OF OPPORTUNITY

The door loomed large and mysterious, its surface adorned with symbols that seemed to shift and change as the group studied them. At its center, a glowing inscription appeared, written in a language none of them recognized, yet they instinctively understood its meaning:

"This door opens not with strength, but with unity; not with force, but with wisdom; not with fear, but with courage."

The message was clear. The door would not yield to any one individual, no matter how strong or capable they were. It required them to work together, to bring forth the lessons they had learned individually and apply them collectively. This was the true test: the final realization that none of them could succeed alone.

Max, standing among the group, looked up at the door with wide eyes. His mind raced back to the time when he had tried to impress Sophie, awkwardly fumbling through his attempts at winning her affection. He had learned that true courage wasn't about bravado; it was about being vulnerable and authentic. That lesson had stuck with him, and now, as he faced the door, he realized that he couldn't open it alone. He needed help, just as he had needed his friends to guide him through his journey with Sophie.

Alina, too, felt the weight of her journey pressing down on her. The Dark Forest had taught her the power of forgiveness, not just of others, but of herself. She had learned that redemption wasn't about erasing the past, but about learning from it and moving forward. The burden of leadership had been heavy on her shoulders, but here, in front of the door, she understood that leadership was not about carrying the weight alone—it was about empowering others to rise alongside her.

As the group stood in silence, each lost in their own thoughts, it was Mia who spoke first. Her voice was steady, but there was an underlying urgency to her words.

"We can't do this alone," she said, her eyes scanning the group. "This door—it's asking for more than just one of us to open it. We need to work together. We need to combine everything we've learned."

The others nodded in agreement, the truth of Mia's words sinking in. They had all faced challenges that had required them to grow, to change, and to adapt. Now, it was time to bring those lessons together.

"But how?" asked Max, his brow furrowed. "How do we open it?"

"The inscription said unity, wisdom, and courage," Alina replied, stepping forward. "We each have something to contribute. We just need to figure out how to use what we've learned."

There was a brief pause as they considered her words. Then, slowly, a plan began to take shape. Each of them would draw upon the lessons they had learned along their journeys and apply them to the door. It wasn't just about physical strength or intelligence; it was about the collective knowledge they had gained through their experiences.

Max was the first to step forward. He had learned that courage was not about acting without fear but about embracing vulnerability. As he approached the door, he placed his hand gently on its surface. For a moment, nothing happened. But then, a soft glow began to emanate from beneath his hand, spreading outwards across the door. It was a small sign, but it was clear that the door had responded to his courage.

Mia stepped forward next. Her journey had been one of questioning societal expectations and finding her own path. She had learned the importance of standing firm in her beliefs and refusing to conform to the pressures of the world around her. As she touched the door, another glow appeared, intertwining with Max's. The door seemed to hum with energy, as if it was recognizing the strength in their combined efforts.

Alina, with her newfound understanding of forgiveness and leadership, was next. She had learned that true leadership wasn't about control—it was about trust, empathy, and collaboration. As she placed her hand on the door, a third glow appeared, merging with the others. The door now pulsed with light, the symbols on its surface shifting and changing as if in response to the collective wisdom they were offering.

One by one, the others stepped forward, each adding their unique lessons to the door. There was Samir, who had learned the value of patience and perseverance in the face of adversity; Elena, who had discovered the power of kindness and empathy; and Marcus, who had realized that sometimes the greatest strength came from asking for help. Each touch, each lesson, brought the door closer to opening.

As the group stood together, their hands on the door, the light grew brighter and brighter until it was almost blinding. But still, the door remained closed. Something was missing.

"It's not enough," Max said, his voice tinged with frustration. "We're doing everything we can, but it's not working."

Alina, her eyes closed in concentration, shook her head. "No, we're missing something. The door isn't just asking for what we've learned individually. It's asking for something more."

Mia's eyes suddenly widened in realization. "Of course! It's not just about us using what we've learned—it's about us working together. We've been thinking about this as individuals, but the door needs us to act as one."

The others looked at her, the truth of her words dawning on them. It wasn't enough to simply apply their individual lessons; they needed to unite their efforts, to synchronize their actions and trust in one another completely. This was the ultimate test—not just of their personal growth, but of their ability to collaborate and trust in each other's strengths.

With a renewed sense of purpose, the group moved closer together, forming a circle around the door. They placed their hands on the surface once more, but this time, they did so with a shared intent. They were no longer thinking of themselves as individuals trying to open the door—they were a collective, a team, each one relying on the others to succeed.

As the group stood united, the door began to change. The glowing symbols on its surface shifted, rearranging themselves into a single, cohesive pattern. The hum of energy grew louder, and the door began to tremble. Slowly, almost imperceptibly at first, the door began to open.

A soft, golden light spilled out from the crack as the door swung wide, revealing what lay beyond. It was not a single, defined destination, but rather a vast expanse of possibility—an endless horizon of potential futures. The air was filled with a sense of freedom and opportunity, as if the world beyond the door was waiting for them to shape it with their actions.

The group stood in awe for a moment, taking in the sight before them. They had done it. Together, they had opened the door.

The lesson of the final door was not just about courage, wisdom, or resilience—it was about the power of unity. Each person had brought their unique experiences and knowledge to the table, but it was only through their collective effort that they had succeeded. The door had not been a test of individual strength or intelligence—it had been a test of their ability to work together, to trust one another, and to use their combined wisdom to unlock the future.

As they stepped through the door, they realized that the journey was far from over. The future was still unwritten, and there would be many more doors to open, many more challenges to face. But now, they knew that they didn't have to face those challenges alone. They had each other, and together, they could overcome anything.

The impossible had become possible—not because of any one person's strength or brilliance, but because they had combined their courage to try, their wisdom to learn, and their resilience to keep going.

As the group disappeared into the light beyond the door, the inscription on its surface glowed one last time, as if imparting a final piece of wisdom:

"Every door leads to another opportunity, if you're willing to open it. Together, we are unstoppable."

And with that, the door closed quietly behind them, leaving only the memory of their journey and the lessons they had learned along the way.

The Open Door

The sun had begun to set, casting a soft, golden glow over the world. It was in this quiet moment that the story found its pause—not an end, but a gentle closing of one chapter and the beginning of another. The door that the characters had opened remained behind them, a symbol of triumph, growth, and the boundless possibilities that lie ahead when courage, wisdom, and unity come together. Each of their journeys had led to this single door, yet it was not the final destination. Rather, it was the beginning of a new journey for them all. The door was open, not just for those who had crossed through it, but for every reader who dared to believe in the possibilities within their own lives.

As each character stepped through the open door, they were no longer the same as when they had begun their individual journeys. Max had transformed from an insecure young man grappling with vulnerability into someone who understood the strength that came from authenticity. Alina had stepped out from the shadows of guilt and self-imposed exile in the Dark Forest, emerging as a leader not through authority, but through humility, understanding, and service. Mia, once bound by the expectations of others, had found her voice and purpose, learning that individuality could coexist harmoniously within a community.

These were only a few of the transformations that had taken place. Each character had faced a door of their own—an obstacle or challenge that had tested their spirit. Some doors had required courage; others, resilience or humility. Each had demanded a leap of faith, a moment of surrender to the unknown. As they now reflected on the path they had traveled, they understood that each door had been an invitation to grow, to learn, and to change. These doors had not simply been barriers to overcome; they had been stepping stones on the path to self-discovery.

For Max, Alina, Mia, and all the others, the journey had been a deeply personal one, yet they had learned that their growth did not occur in isolation. By stepping through each door, they had not only transformed themselves but had also paved the way for others. Their journeys illuminated a path, showing others that it was possible to find courage, wisdom, and unity in even the most challenging situations. The door they had opened was not just a physical one; it was a symbol of every opportunity, every chance to begin again, every lesson to be learned, and every person to be helped along the way.

The open door, with its gentle light spilling into the future, remained a powerful symbol of opportunity. It represented all the doors each of us encounters in life: the door of choice, of possibility, of change. Some doors we step through willingly, excited to see what lies on the other side; others we avoid, fearful of the unknown they represent. But in the end, every door holds within it the potential to transform us. It is an invitation to leave behind what is comfortable, to explore, to learn, and to grow.

The door also reminded each of the characters of the endless nature of these opportunities. While the door was a culmination of their shared journey, it also reminded them that life would continue to present them with new doors to open, new paths to explore, and new lessons to learn. Each door they encountered would require the skills and wisdom they had gained from their previous experiences. There would be new challenges, but they were no longer afraid; they knew now that each door led to growth, to greater understanding, and to connection with others who shared similar journeys.

In the same way, the open door invites every reader to consider the possibilities in their own lives. It encourages each person to reflect on the doors they have already opened and to recognize those that still await them. For some, these doors might represent career changes or new relationships; for others, they might represent personal healing, creative expression, or the pursuit of lifelong dreams. Every door, no matter how intimidating it might seem, offers an opportunity for transformation.

The narrator extends this invitation to the reader, inviting them to pause and look at the doors in their own life. Perhaps there is a door they have been afraid to open, a chance they have been hesitant to take. Perhaps there is a door they walked through long ago, one that led them to an unexpected yet profoundly rewarding destination. Or maybe there is a door just ahead, waiting patiently, ready to reveal new opportunities.

The open door is not just for the characters in this story; it is for everyone. It stands as a reminder that life is full of choices, full of possibilities, and that each person has the power to shape their own journey. For every door that seems daunting, there is an equal measure of strength within each person to face it. Sometimes, all it takes is the courage to take the first step, the willingness to trust oneself, and the belief that, no matter how dark the path may seem, there is always light on the other side.

For those who may feel stuck, unsure, or fearful, the door represents a message of hope. It is a gentle reminder that it is never too late to change course, to start over, or to pursue a dream that once seemed impossible. Life's doors do not close forever; they wait, silently offering second chances, new beginnings, and the possibility of a different future. In opening each door, we choose to grow, to heal, and to become more fully ourselves.

The journey of the characters in this story also speaks to the power of collective strength. While each of them faced individual challenges, it was their ability to come together, to trust one another, and to unite their strengths that ultimately allowed them to open the door. This serves as a powerful reminder that we do not have to walk through life's doors alone. There is strength in community, in friendship, and in shared experiences. When we come together, we create a support system that can help us face even the most difficult challenges.

The open door invites each of us to consider how we might help others on their journeys. Just as the characters supported one another, we, too, can play a role in helping others open the doors in their lives. Whether it is through words of encouragement, acts of kindness, or simply being present, we have the power to make a difference in someone else's life. By lifting each other up, by offering guidance and support, we become part of a collective strength that is far greater than any individual effort. The open door reminds us that we are all connected and that, together, we can accomplish things that would be impossible alone.

As the characters walked through the door, they stepped into a world of infinite possibility. This vision reminds us that life is full of potential, full of dreams waiting to be realized. The open door represents not just a single opportunity, but a lifetime of chances to grow, to explore, and to find fulfillment. It is an invitation to embrace life in all its uncertainty and to trust that, with every door we open, we move closer to understanding ourselves and the world around us.

As the sun finally set, casting a warm, golden light over the open door, the characters felt a deep sense of peace and fulfillment. They had faced their fears, conquered their doubts, and had grown in ways they had never imagined. They knew that there would be more doors to open, more challenges to face, but they were ready. They had learned that the journey was just as important as the destination and that every step forward was a victory in itself.

The open door invites us all to embrace the journey, to cherish each moment, and to find joy in the process of growth. It reminds us that life is a series of doors, each one offering a new lesson, a new adventure, or *a new beginning. As we walk through each door, we become more fully ourselves, more resilient, and more compassionate.*

In the end, the open door is a symbol of hope, courage, and possibility. It reminds us that life is full of opportunities and that, no matter where we are or what we have been through, there is always a path forward. It is an invitation to trust in the journey, to believe in ourselves, and to find strength in the support of those around us.

As we close the final chapter, let us carry with us the lessons of the journey—the courage to face our fears, the wisdom to learn from our experiences, and the resilience to keep going. And let us remember that, no matter how many doors we have already opened, there are always more waiting for us. Each door leads to another opportunity, another chance to grow, and another step toward becoming the person we are meant to be.

With a deep breath and a hopeful heart, let us look forward to the open doors in our own lives, ready to step through and see what lies on the other side. For every door, every challenge, and every journey, there is a world of infinite possibility, waiting to be discovered.

Don't miss out!

Visit the website below and you can sign up to receive emails whenever Smita Singh publishes a new book. There's no charge and no obligation.

https://books2read.com/r/B-A-LYEOB-JPUDF

BOOKS 2 READ

Connecting independent readers to independent writers.

Did you love *Beyond the Impossible – Doors of Opportunity*? Then you should read *Mahadev: My Encounter with Shiva*[1] by Smita Singh!

Welcome to "Mahadev: My Encounter with Shiva." This book is the result of a deeply personal and spiritual journey, one that began as a quest for understanding the mysteries of life, purpose, and the divine. Like many of us, I have always been drawn to the big questions—Why are we here? What is the meaning of life? Is there something greater that guides us through the ups and downs of our existence? These questions have echoed in my heart for years, and this book is my way of exploring those profound inquiries.

As the narrator meditates for years and finally meets Lord Shiva, we are invited into a dialogue that transcends time and space. The questions asked in these pages are ones we all carry within us—questions about

---

1. https://books2read.com/u/mBBqnv

2. https://books2read.com/u/mBBqnv

life, death, love, fear, and enlightenment. In this tale, Shiva answers with the ancient wisdom of the cosmos, providing insights that challenge our perceptions and open our hearts to new possibilities.

This book is not just about seeking answers from the divine—it is about a journey inward. It's about finding the sacred within ourselves and recognizing the interconnectedness of all life. I hope that as you walk alongside the narrator on this path, you will discover your own truths and connect with the deeper, spiritual dimensions of existence.

Shiva, as the Lord of Transformation, represents change, renewal, and the balance between creation and destruction. In the same way, this book is meant to be a tool for transformation—a guide to help you reflect on your own life, your purpose, and the greater forces at play in the universe.

As you turn the pages, I encourage you to approach this book with an open mind and an open heart. The journey is not just the narrator's, it's yours too. Each question, each answer, is an opportunity to look within and contemplate the divine wisdom that surrounds us all.